This book is dedicated to our beloved princesses—Catherine, Alexandra, Danika, Emmalynn, and Megan—and our fearless princes—Christian, Zachary, Payton, Maverick, and Christopher. May you realize your royal place in the kingdom and grow to be dynamic daughters and sons for the King.

To every parent of a princess, we invite you to capture the heart of your child with our inspiring character-building parables. May she aspire to be a daughter of the King from our little princesses in this story.

J.Y. and J.J.

Dedicated to my father . . .

O.A.

ZONDERKIDZ

Princess Joy's Birthday Blessing
Copyright © 2011 by Jeanna Young and Jacqueline Johnson
Illustrations © 2011 by Omar Aranda

Requests for information should be addressed to:
Zonderkidz, *Grand Rapids, Michigan 49530*

Library of Congress Cataloging-in-Publication Data
Young, Jeanna Stolle, 1968-
    Princess Joy's birthday blessing / by Jeanna Stolle Young and Jacqueline
Kinney Johnson ; [illustrations by Omar Aranda].
        p.   cm.
    Summary: When none of the princes or princesses from neighboring
kingdoms is able to attend Princess Joy's birthday party, she asks the King if she
can invite children from the village, instead, in this version of the parable of the
wedding guests. Includes note about the parable and its meaning for children.
    ISBN 978-0-310-71639-6 (hardcover)
    [1. Princesses—Fiction. 2. Birthdays—Fiction. 3. Generosity—Fiction. 4.
Christian life—Fiction. 5. Parables.] I. Johnson, Jacqueline Kinney, 1943- II.
Aranda, Omar, ill. III. Title.
PZ7.Y8654Prj 2011
[E]—dc22
                              2010002000

All Scripture quotations unless otherwise noted are taken from the Holy Bible, *New International Version*®, *NIV*®. Copyright © 1973, 1978, 1984 by Biblica, Inc.™ Used by permission of Zondervan. All rights reserved worldwide.

Any Internet addresses (websites, blogs, etc.) and telephone numbers printed in this book are offered as a resource. They are not intended in any way to be or imply an endorsement by Zondervan, nor does Zondervan vouch for the content of these sites and numbers for the life of this book.

All rights reserved. No part of this publication may be reproduced, stored in a re-trieval system, or transmitted in any form or by any means—electronic, mechanical, photocopy, recording, or any other—except for brief quotations in printed reviews, without the prior permission of the publisher.

Zonderkidz is a trademark of Zondervan.

The Princess Parables is a trademark of Zondervan.

Editor: Mary Hassinger
Art direction & design: Kris Nelson

Printed in China

---

11 12 13 14 15 / LPC / 22 21 20 19 18 17 16 15 14 13 12 11 10 9 8 7 6 5 4 3 2 1

The Princess Parables™

Princess Joy's
Birthday Blessing

WRITTEN BY **Jeanna Young** & **Jacqueline Johnson**
ILLUSTRATED BY **Omar Aranda**

ZONDERVAN.com/
AUTHORTRACKER
follow your favorite authors

Once upon a time, in a magnificent castle perched high on a hill above the sea, there lived five princesses. Their names were Joy, Grace, Faith, Hope, and Charity. They were blessed to be the daughters of the king.

This is the story of Princess Joy. She walks with a skip in her step. She is a smile on a cloudy day. She loves fluffy dresses, shimmering ribbons in her hair, and sparkly shoes. She is often found daydreaming about fairy tales and fancy festivities … like her quickly approaching birthday!

As the morning sun sprinkled a confetti illumination across Princess Joy's bedroom, she was awakened by her favorite puppy, Rosebud. She smiled while hugging his neck and said, "Only ten more days until my birthday!"

Bounding from the bed, Princess Joy heard her sisters' voices rising and falling in excitement throughout the courtyard below. She tiptoed to the window listening closely.

"We will decorate everything in pink since it's her favorite color," said Princess Hope. "Pink balloons, pink streamers, pink roses."

"Maybe Daddy will let us use the best china," said Princess Grace.

"Let's serve cotton-candy punch, strawberry ice cream, and rainbow cookies," said Princess Faith. "We can't forget chocolate petit fours and an enormous tiered cake with sparkling pink frosting!"

"SHHH! Remember this is a surprise!" Princess Hope reminded them.

Princess Joy's heart leapt as she heard the news. She danced her quiet happy dance with Rosebud, imagining the party in her mind. As excited as she was, she felt genuinely loved by the thoughtfulness of her sisters.

Beautiful invitations were sent to princes and princesses in faraway lands. In anticipation of the upcoming day, the sisters planned a wonderful celebration!

Happy
Birthday
to
Princess Joy

You are Invited
to a
Royal Celebration!

Please join us for
Princess Joy's
Birthday Party!
Saturday at 1:00
at the
King's Palace

Soon the responses to the invitations began to arrive. No one could come. Not even one! They all had excuses. Prince Jack was invited to a different party. Princess Ashlynn had just gotten a new bike and wanted to ride it. Princess Elizabeth had a new baby brother and needed to stay home with her mother. The list went on and on.

"No one can come to the surprise party, Daddy. What will we do?" Princess Faith asked.

The king turned to see Rosebud appear. Tiptoeing toward the window with a finger to his lips, and making a gesture to silence the girls, they heard crying.

Slowly, the king pulled back the curtain to find Princess Joy. Looking into his compassionate face, she said, "I don't want them to come to my party. It doesn't matter if anyone comes!"

"Listen, Joy, those who were invited first are missing out, but there may be a better plan. Don't worry. You may still be surprised!" the king declared.

Later, as the sun set, Princess Joy sat at the edge of the courtyard, watching her sisters and father singing and dancing around the fountain.

She smiled to herself and said, "Daddy and my sisters ARE a party!" Her disappointment about her birthday instantly changed to happiness.

Just then, Princess Joy peered through the twilight and saw a little girl. She was smiling.

Joy jumped up and ran to the king. "I would like to invite the children who don't live in a castle or a nice house. Let's invite the boys and girls who don't have a fancy bike or big birthday parties. Let's invite the children in our village."

The king grinned. It was exactly what he had hoped Joy would do. "My dear Joy," he said, "you will be blessed at this birthday party, more than all the others." As she pondered his words, she wondered, *What does Daddy mean?*

Invitations were sent again. The princesses all hoped the children would not refuse.

The princesses were overjoyed at the response, especially Joy. This time everyone they invited was coming to the birthday party. The sisters began to prepare—baking cakes, making party favors, picking flowers, and so on.

Soon the day of the party arrived, and the guests began to line up at the castle— each with a gift from the heart! Some came with beautiful wildflower bouquets and hand-painted pictures, others with embroidered hankies and baskets of homemade goodies. Joy was awestruck by the generosity of their hearts.

The children played games, drank punch, sang songs, and watched puppet shows. When the time came, the baker presented a gigantic, pink, tiered cake with sparkling candles. Princess Joy blew out the candles while her new friends watched. She was blessed by their inner beauty and kindness and wondered why she had never thought of this before.

Birthdays mean presents and presents Joy got! The king and princesses entered the room carrying elegantly wrapped presents in every size imaginable. But rather than Princess Joy getting the gifts, she had the best idea yet. She leaned over and whispered something in her father's ear.

In response, the king lifted Princess Joy onto his throne and announced that each child would take turns sitting next to her while Princess Joy gave gifts to each one of her new friends. It was the grandest birthday party of all time!

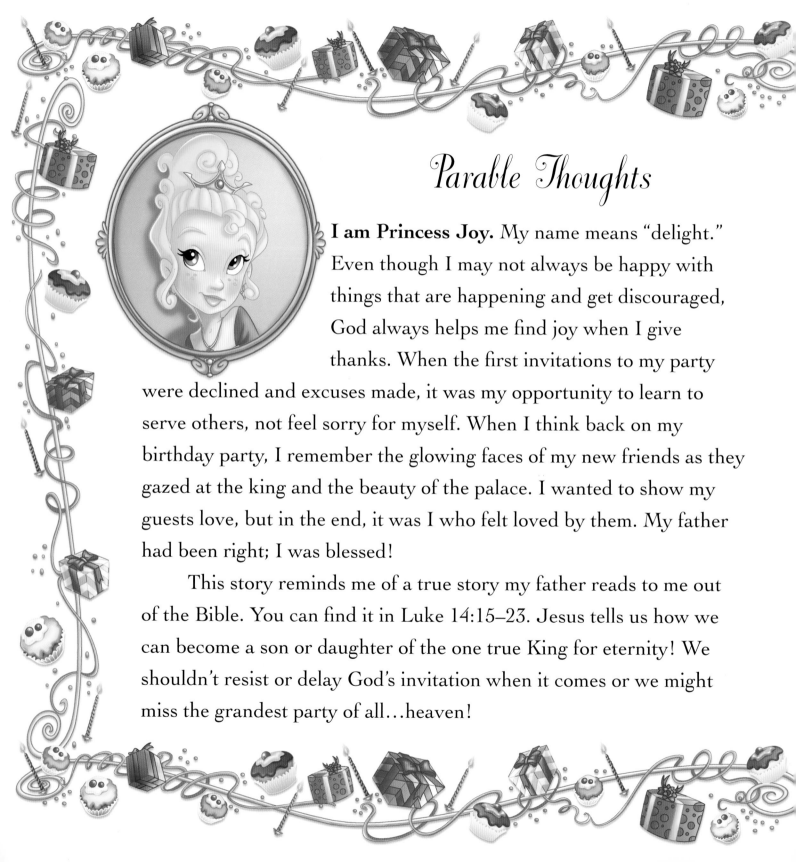

Parable Thoughts

I am Princess Joy. My name means "delight." Even though I may not always be happy with things that are happening and get discouraged, God always helps me find joy when I give thanks. When the first invitations to my party were declined and excuses made, it was my opportunity to learn to serve others, not feel sorry for myself. When I think back on my birthday party, I remember the glowing faces of my new friends as they gazed at the king and the beauty of the palace. I wanted to show my guests love, but in the end, it was I who felt loved by them. My father had been right; I was blessed!

This story reminds me of a true story my father reads to me out of the Bible. You can find it in Luke 14:15–23. Jesus tells us how we can become a son or daughter of the one true King for eternity! We shouldn't resist or delay God's invitation when it comes or we might miss the grandest party of all…heaven!

Then Jesus spoke to his host. "Suppose you give a lunch or dinner," he said. "Do not invite your friends, your brothers or sisters, or your relative, or your rich neighbors. If you do, they may invite you to eat with them. So you will be paid back. But when you give a big dinner, invite those who are poor. Also invite those who can't walk, the disabled and the blind. Then you will be blessed. Your guests can't pay you back. But you will be paid back when those who are right with God rise from the dead."

LUKE 14:12–14 (NIrV)